DINOSAURS ARE DIFFERENT

by ALIKI

THOMAS Y. CROWELL • NEW YORK

Other *Let's-Read-and-Find-Out Science Books®* by Aliki

Corn Is Maize • Digging Up Dinosaurs • Fossils Tell of Long Ago
Green Grass and White Milk • The Long-Lost Coelacanth and Other Living Fossils
My Five Senses • My Hands • My Visit to the Dinosaurs • Wild and Woolly Mammoths

for David and Adrian Lagakos

With thanks to Kathleen Zoehfeld and to William F. Simpson, Chief Preparator of
Fossil Vertebrates, Field Museum of Natural History, for their kind help.

The *Let's-Read-and-Find-Out Science Book* series was originated by Dr. Franklyn M. Branley, Astronomer Emeritus
and former Chairman of The American Museum-Hayden Planetarium, and was formerly co-edited by him and Dr.
Roma Gans, Professor Emeritus of Childhood Education, Teachers College, Columbia University. For a complete
catalog of Let's-Read-and-Find-Out Science Books, write to Thomas Y. Crowell Junior Books, Harper & Row,
Publishers, Inc., 10 East 53rd Street, New York, NY 10022.

Dinosaurs Are Different
Copyright © 1985 by Aliki Brandenberg
Printed in the U.S.A.   All rights reserved.

Library of Congress Cataloging in Publication Data
Aliki.
    Dinosaurs are different.

    (Let's-read-and-find-out science book)
    Summary: Explains how the various orders and
suborders of dinosaurs were similar and different
in structure and appearance.
    1. Dinosaurs—Juvenile literature. [1. Dinosaurs]
I. Title. II. Series.
QE862.D5A343 1985   567.9'1   84-45332
ISBN 0-690-04456-9   ISBN 0-690-04458-5 (lib. bdg.)

5 6 7 8 9 10

DINOSAURS ARE DIFFERENT

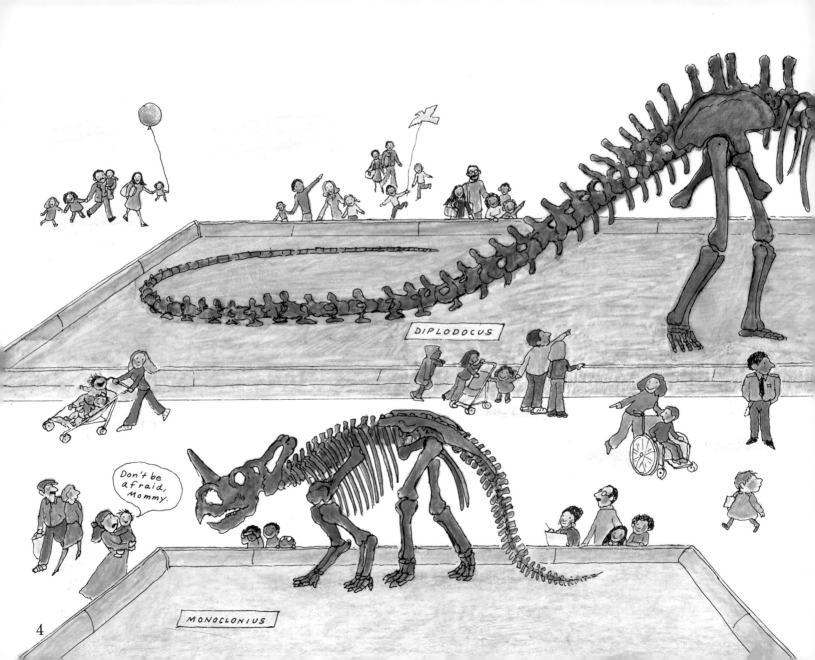

DIPLODOCUS

MONOCLONIUS

Don't be afraid, Mommy.

4

I like to visit the dinosaurs.
I like to study their skeletons.
I have found out a lot about dinosaurs
by looking at their bones.

5

The minute I saw *Tyrannosaurus*,
I knew it was a meat-eater.
A meat-eater's teeth are long and pointy.
But *Iguanodon* could never chew meat.
Its teeth are too flat.
They were made for crushing and grinding plants.

IGUANODON

TYRANNOSAURUS

What's THAT?

His hip bone, of course.

I noticed something else.
Look at their hips.
Tyrannosaurus has a big bone pointing forward.
Iguanodon doesn't.

CAMARASAURUS

HYPSILOPHODON

That one is like Tyrannosaurus.

I thought all dinosaurs were big.

This one has hips like Iguanodon.

8

I looked at other skeletons.
I saw that some dinosaurs have hips
like *Tyrannosaurus.*
Others have hips like *Iguanodon.*
I wondered what this meant.
I soon found out.
Dinosaurs are different.

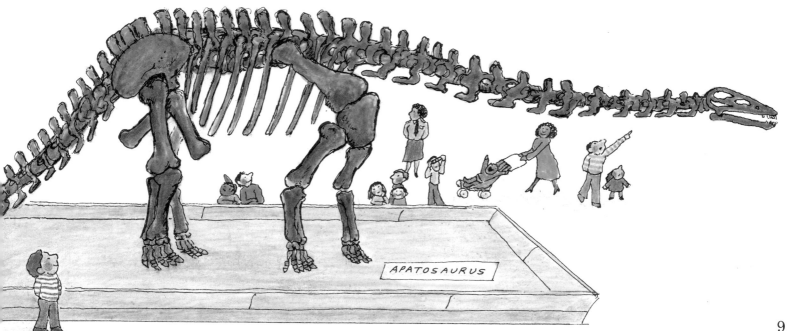

APATOSAURUS

Tyrannosaurus and *Iguanodon* were cousins.
Each belonged to a different order of dinosaurs.
Tyrannosaurus was a SAURISCHIAN dinosaur.
Iguanodon was an ORNITHISCHIAN dinosaur.
Saurischia and ornithischia belong to
a larger group called ARCHOSAURIA—"ruling reptiles."
There were others in the archosaur group—
THECODONTS, CROCODILIANS, and PTEROSAURS.
But there were more dinosaurs than other archosaurs.
Dinosaurs ruled the earth for 140 million years.

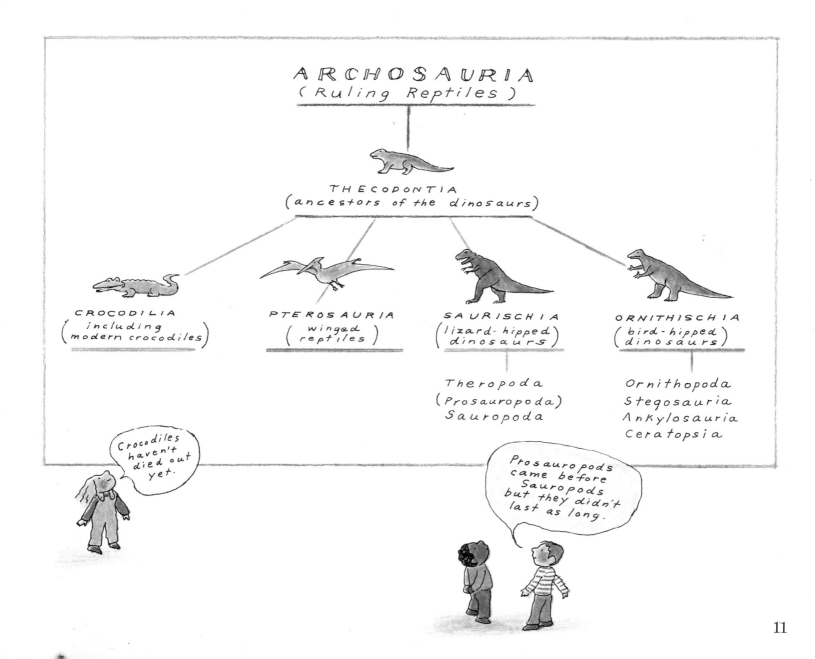

11

All dinosaurs are either saurischians or ornithischians.
They are divided into these two separate orders
because they have different structures.
One big difference between the two groups
is their hips.

13

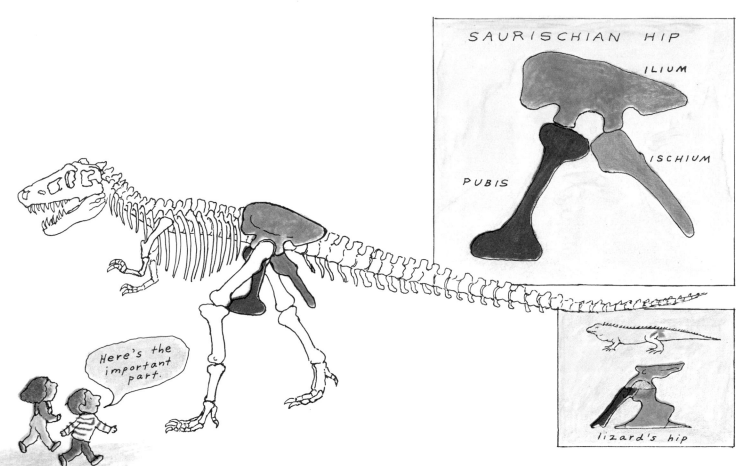

Saurischians are "lizard-hipped" dinosaurs.
They have hips like other reptiles.
One pelvic bone points forward.
The other points backward.

Ornithischians are "bird-hipped" dinosaurs.
They have hips more like a bird's.
Both pelvic bones point in the same direction—
backward.

Their jawbones are different, too.
A saurischian has a dentary—
a main jawbone that holds the teeth.
So do other reptiles.
But an ornithischian has an extra beaklike bone
in front of its teeth called a predentary.
No other reptile has a predentary.

These clues help us tell saurischian dinosaurs from ornithischian dinosaurs. But you can be fooled. Even dinosaurs belonging to the same order are different.

The saurischians are divided into two suborders—SAUROPODA and THEROPODA.
Most of the sauropods were plant-eaters. Most were gigantic, and they all walked on four legs.

SAURISCHIA

SAUROPODA

DIPLODOCUS
90 feet long
20,000 pounds

APATOSAURUS
70 feet long
70,000 pounds

19

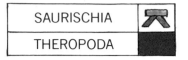
Theropods all walked on two legs.
All of them ate meat.
Coelurosaurs were small theropods.

Deinonychosaurs were clawed theropods.

Carnosaurs were the giant theropods.
They were the fiercest of all.

TYRANNOSAURUS
40 feet long
15,000 pounds

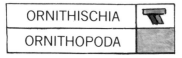

ORNITHISCHIA	
ORNITHOPODA	

There were different kinds of ornithischians, too.
They are divided into four suborders—
ORNITHOPODA, CERATOPSIA, STEGOSAURIA,
and ANKYLOSAURIA.
Ornithopods had two strong legs.
They could run very fast from their enemies...

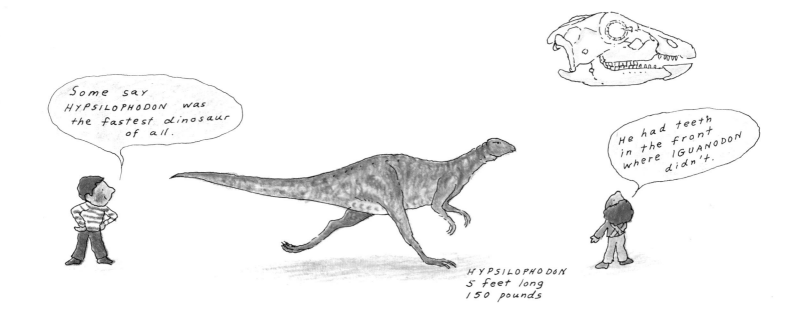

Some say HYPSILOPHODON was the fastest dinosaur of all.

He had teeth in the front where IGUANODON didn't.

HYPSILOPHODON
5 feet long
150 pounds

...or they could swat them with a forceful tail.

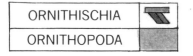
Hadrosaurs were duck-billed ornithopods.
Duckbills had hundreds of teeth and a flat beak.
They had webbed feet, and strong tails
shaped like paddles, to help them swim.
Crested duckbills had bony crests on top
of their heads.

ANATOSAURUS
30 feet long
6,700 pounds

webbed
fingers

CORYTHOSAURUS
30 feet long
9,000 pounds

24

Psittacosaurs and *Pachycephalosaurs*
were ornithopods, too.
Psittacosaurus had a parrotlike beak.
Pachycephalosaur was a dome-headed dinosaur.

PSITTACOSAURUS
6 feet long
55 pounds

PSITTACOSAURUS
was small and
slow, and
there's
its beak!

That's a thick,
lumpy skull you
have there,
PACHYCEPHALOSAURUS.

PACHYCEPHALOSAURUS
20 feet long
2,000 pounds

The rest of the ornithischians—ceratopsians,
stegosaurs, and ankylosaurs—
all walked on four legs.
They all had tough skin and bony protection.
Ceratopsians were horned dinosaurs.

3 deadly horns and a big, bony collar.

A lot to carry around.

SOME PROTECTION!

TRICERATOPS
25 feet long
18,000 pounds

Stegosaurs were plated dinosaurs.

STEGOSAURUS
20 feet long
5,000 pounds

Ankylosaurs were armored dinosaurs.

ANKYLOSAURUS
15 feet long
4,000 pounds

These had bony armor.

And dangerous tails, I see.

I bet not even the King wanted to take a bite.

Ugh.

SCOLOSAURUS
20 feet long
6,000 pounds

SCOLOSAURUS

Horned, plated, and armored dinosaurs
were clumsy and slow.
They could not outrun their enemies.
But who would want to get too close?
Not I.
And I don't have to worry.
Dinosaurs died out 65 million years ago.
But I'm glad they left their bones behind.
That's how we know so much about them.

Goodbye!

Bye.

Thanks
for the
guided
tour!

See
you
next
time.

ARCHOSAURIA
(Ruling Reptiles)

 SAURISCHIA
(lizard-hip)

 SAUROPODA

Apatosaurus
Camarasaurus
Diplodocus

THEROPODA

Coelurosauria
Coelophysis
Deinonychosauria
Deinonychus
Carnosauria
Tyrannosaurus

 ORNITHISCHIA
(bird-hip)

ORTHINOPODA

Hypsilophodon
Iguanodon
Pachycephalosaurus
Psittacosaurus
Hadrosauria
Anatosaurus
Corythosaurus

CERATOPSIA

Monoclonius
Triceratops

STEGOSAURIA

Stegosaurus

ANKYLOSAURIA

Ankylosaurus
Scolosaurus

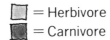
= Herbivore
= Carnivore